IMAGINE THAT

Licensed exclusively to Imagine That Publishing Ltd
Tide Mill Way, Woodbridge, Suffolk, IP12 1AP, UK
www.imaginethat.com
Copyright © 2021 Imagine That Group Ltd
All rights reserved
0 2 4 6 8 9 7 5 3 1
Manufactured in China

Written by Joshua George
Illustrated by Rosie Butcher

ISBN 978-1-78958-612-1

A catalogue record for this book is available from the British Library

The Pied Piper of Hamelin

Adapted by Joshua George

Illustrated by Rosie Butcher

The river Weser, deep and wide,
Flows by Hamelin's wall on the southern side.
A pleasanter spot you never spied,
But listen, voices, what's that they cried?

HAMELIN TOWN

They fought the dogs and killed the cats,
And ate the cheeses out of the vats.
And licked the soup from the cook's own ladles,
And bit the babies in the cradles!

In the town hall the Mayor spoke up,
'What we need is some kind of trap!'
Just as he said this who should rap,
At the wooden door with a gentle tap?

'Bless me,' cried the Mayor, 'what's that?
Only a scraping of shoes on the mat?
Anything like the sound of a rat
Makes my heart go pit-a-pat!'

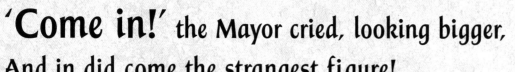

'**Come in!**' the Mayor cried, looking bigger,
And in did come the strangest figure!
His weird long coat from heel to head
Was half of yellow and half of red,

There stood a man both **tall and thin**,
With sharp blue eyes, each like a pin,
And lips where smiles went out and in,
A most peculiar looking thing!

He walked up to the Mayor's table
'I've come to tell you,' said he, 'I'm able,
By means of a secret song to charm
All animals from where they cause harm,
Any living creature beneath the sun,
That creeps, or swims, or flies or runs,
And people call me the **Pied Piper!**

I hear your troubles, see your frowns,
If I charm the rats out of your town,
Will you pay me a thousand crowns?'
'One? **Fifty thousand!**' said the Mayor in his gown.

Into the street the **Piper** stepped,
And before three notes his lips had left,
A noise was heard like an army muttering,
And the muttering grew to a grumbling,
And the grumbling grew to a mighty rumbling ...

And out of the houses the **rats** came tumbling!
Great **rats**, small **rats**, lean **rats**, brawny **rats**,
Brown **rats**, black **rats**, grey **rats**, tawny **rats**.
He led them all to the River Weser,
Where the **rats** plunged in, and were gone forever!

You should have heard the Hamelin people,
Ringing the bells till they rocked the steeple!
'**Come on,**' cried the Mayor, '**let's celebrate,**
Let's eat too much and stay up too late.

Fetch the musicians and the clowns!'
When suddenly the Mayor saw the face
Of the Piper appear in the market-place,
'But first, if you please, my thousand crowns!'

'A thousand crowns!' The Mayor looked blue,
And all the townsfolk looked blue too!
'Wait,' said the Mayor with a cunning wink,
'Our business was done at the river's brink,
We saw with our eyes the rats all sink,
And what's dead can't come to life, I think.
But a thousand crowns? Come, take fifty!'
The Mayor was acting very shifty!

The **Piper's** face grew dark, his eyes bright,
'We had a bargain, this is not right!
And you'll find that those who do not pay

Will hear me pipe a different way!'

'**What?**' cried the Mayor,
'Do you think you can
Treat me like a normal man?
You threaten us, Piper? Do your worst,
Blow your pipe until you burst!'

Once more the **Piper** stepped in the street,
And before three notes his lips had left,
Small feet were pattering, wooden shoes clattering,
Little hands clapping and little tongues chattering,
And, like farm-yard hens when barley's scattering ...

Out came the little boys and girls,
With rosy cheeks and golden curls,
And sparkling eyes and teeth like pearls.
Tripping and skipping, they ran merrily after
The wonderful music with shouting and laughter.

The Mayor and all the people stood,
As if they were changed into blocks of wood,
While out of Hamelin, the Piper went advancing,
With the children following, clapping and dancing.

Until they came to a mountain side,
When, with a loud 'crack', it opened wide,
And when all were gone from sound and sight,
The mountain groaned, and then shut tight!

'Let's pay what we owe!' the Mayor cried,
And people brought money from low and high,
And gathered together as the clock struck three,
The thousand crowns for the Piper's fee.

'If we take the money to the mountain crack,
The **Piper** might bring our children back.'
So before dusk fell the bag was there,
And the townspeople waited in the market-square.

The hours passed, the town fell quiet,
'Sshhh,' whispered the Mayor, 'what was that?'

A high pitched sound like distant singing,
A tumbling sound like church bells ringing,
There in the distance, the children coming!

The Mayor signed a decree with his special quill pen,
What we owe, we'll pay, there and then!